The Day the Teacher Went Bananas

The Day the Teacher Went Bananas

by James Howe

illustrated by Lillian Hoban

Viking Kestrel

VIKING KESTREL

Penguin Books Ltd, Harmondsworth, Middlesex, England
Viking Penguin Inc., 40 West 23rd Street, New York, New York 10010, U.S.A.
Penguin Books Australia Ltd, Ringwood, Victoria, Australia
Penguin Books Canada Ltd, 2801 John Street, Markham, Ontario, Canada L3R 1B4
Penguin Books (N.Z.) Ltd, 182–190 Wairau Road, Auckland 10, New Zealand

First published in the United States, 1984, by E. P. Dutton, Inc.,
2 Park Avenue, New York, N.Y. 10016
First published in Great Britain, 1985

ISBN 0-670-80340-5
Editor: Ann Durell   Designer: Isabel Warren-Lynch
Printed in Hong Kong by South China Printing Co.

for my mother

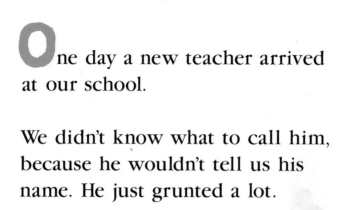

One day a new teacher arrived
at our school.

We didn't know what to call him,
because he wouldn't tell us his
name. He just grunted a lot.

When it was time for arithmetic, he showed us how to count on our toes.

And we learned a new way to write.

We went outside for science class.

Then we went back inside for lunch.
The teacher ate sixteen bananas.

"Tomorrow, let's bring bananas for
lunch," we all said, wanting to be
just like our new teacher.

Then we had art class. Our teacher
taught us how to work with clay.

And paper.

And paint.

Then we studied music.

Suddenly, Mr. Hornsby, the school principal, came into the room with another man.

"There has been a terrible mix-up,"
Mr. Hornsby said. "This isn't
your new teacher. This is
a gorilla."

The man with Mr. Hornsby said, "I am your new teacher. My name is Mr. Quackerbottom. I was sent to the zoo by mistake."

Sadly, we all waved good-bye
to the gorilla.

"Now," Mr. Quackerbottom said, "what have you learned today?"

We showed him.

"Why, this is awful!" Mr. Quackerbottom
cried. "You all belong in the zoo!"

And the next day, that's exactly where we went...

... to have lunch with our
favourite teacher.